World Myths & Tales

CAROLYN SWIFT

Children's
POOLBEG

For Lena

Because I told all the Irish and European myths for her, so I may as well tell these for her too.

First published in 1993 by
Poolbeg,
A division of Poolbeg Enterprises Ltd,
Knocksedan House,
Swords, Co. Dublin, Ireland.

© Carolyn Swift 1993

The moral right of the author has been asserted.

A catalogue record for this book is available from the British Library.

ISBN 1 85371 295 7

Cover illustration by Angela Clarke
Cover design by Poolbeg Group Services Ltd
Set by Mac Book Limited in Stone 10/14
Printed by The Guernsey Press Limited,
Vale, Guernsey, Channel Islands.

Contents

ABOUT THIS BOOK

I have called this book *World Myths and Tales* because the stories in it come from all over the world, but of course there are many countries with wonderful stories that are not included here. Some were left out on purpose, like Ireland and the other countries of western Europe, because many of them were included in my two earlier collections, but Finland, Russia and a whole lot of other countries from eastern Europe and Asia should have been amongst these. Maybe one day they may have another book all to themselves. There are also forty-five different countries in Africa and I have only been able to fit in stories from two: one Arab (Egypt) in the north-eastern tip and one black (the tiny country of Lesotho) right down in the south.

The stories I have included, however, often come from a number of different countries. The story of *Rama*, for instance, is told and danced wherever there are Hindus, not only in India but in places as far away as Vietnam or Bali, while the story of *Sedna* is known to the Inuit people, whether they live in Canada, Alaska, Greenland or Siberia. As for Maui's adventures, they are told not only amongst the Maoris of New Zealand but also in many of the hundreds of islands in the Pacific Ocean like Hawaii, Tahiti, Samoa, Fiji and Tonga.

But the important thing is not where the stories come from but the exciting tales they tell and the explanations they give of our world and how it came to be the way it is today, tales told by people long ago with great imaginations who knew less than we do about some things but maybe a whole lot more about others.

Carolyn Swift
1993

❖

The Sun, the Looking-Glass and
the Eight-Headed Dragon

❖

Japan

❖

Back in the mists of time there lived a boy called Susanoo. His father and mother were the first people on earth, but then his father became Lord of the Heavens and his mother Lady of the Underworld.

Susanoo himself lived with his brothers and sisters on the bridge which linked heaven and earth, but he was always complaining. He complained about not being able to visit his mother, even though his father explained to him that if he once went to the underworld he would never be able to come back, and he complained even more when his sister Amaterasu was given the jewelled necklace of heaven and made goddess of the sun, while he was given only corals and made god of the sea. Finally his father became sick of his constant moanings and groanings.

"I don't want to see your face around Heaven any more," he told him. "You have the whole earth and sea to play around in so there's no need for you to make all our lives a misery up here."

"Oh, all right," Susanoo grumbled, "but first I must say goodbye to Amaterasu."

So off he stumped to look for her. Being in a bad mood, he shook every mountain he passed so that rocks crashed down the slopes, and he stamped his feet so that the earth quaked. Hearing all the noise, Amaterasu was frightened. She took up her bow and arrow so that, when her younger brother arrived, he found himself facing the drawn bow of a fierce-looking warrior.

"You can put that thing down," he told her. "I come in peace."

"Prove it," she said suspiciously, not taking her eyes off him.

Susanoo handed her his sword. She took it from him and broke it into three pieces. Then, before he could complain, she blew on them and turned them into three beautiful little girls.

"One day these three little daughters of mine will bring new life into the world," she told him, "while your sword could only have brought death."

"I can do better than that!" Susanoo boasted. "Give me the necklaces you're wearing."

So Amaterasu unclasped the five necklaces and gave them to her brother. Then he blew on them and turned them into five little boys.

"Now I have five sons," he said.

"They were made out of *my* necklaces so they should be *my* sons!" Amaterasu snapped.

"But your daughters were made from *my* sword," Susanoo argued.

"That's different!" Amaterasu told him.

At that Susanoo lost his temper. He tore up all the rice fields that Amaterasu had been carefully ripening and caused such destruction that the frightened goddess ran and hid in a cave, blocking the entrance with a large stone.

Because Amaterasu was the sun goddess, this meant that the world was suddenly plunged into darkness. Without the sun's heat the land became very cold and nothing grew in field or forest. Worse still, the evil spirits took advantage of the darkness to get up to all sorts of wickedness. It was a disaster. Something had to be done, so all the good spirits gathered together in a dry river bed to try to decide what to do.

"We must tempt Amaterasu to come out of the cave," said one.

"And block up the entrance the minute she does, so she can't go back into it again," added another.

"But what would tempt her to come out?" asked a third.

"We must put everything she likes most outside," replied the first.

"And what *does* she like most?" the third asked.

"Seeing her sunny face reflected in the lake," answered a fourth.

"But we can't bring the lake up to the cave!" objected the third.

"Then we must make something that will reflect

her face the way the lake does and put _that_ outside the cave," suggested a fifth.

"I don't know what we could make that would do that," the third grumbled, "and anyway, how will she know it's there unless we can get her to come out of the cave in the first place?"

At that they all looked thoughtful. No one spoke for a while.

"I know!" the second suddenly shouted in triumph. "She always used to come out every morning as soon as she heard the cock crow. We must get all the cocks to crow outside the cave."

So they all put their heads together to try to think what would reflect the sun like the waters of the lake. After trying all sort of things in vain, they finally managed to invent a mirror, or looking-glass. This they hung from the branch of a japonica tree immediately opposite the cave and, knowing Amaterasu's fondness for jewellery, they hung jewelled necklaces from the other branches.

When all was ready, they gathered outside the cave with every cock they could find. First they chanted prayers. Then they gave the signal and all the cocks began to crow. Not satisfied with that, everyone present began to sing and dance, led by the goddess Ama no Uzume doing a tap-dance on an upturned tub.

Wondering what all the noise was about, Amaterasu peeped out of the cave and at once saw her own face reflected in the mirror. She had never seen a looking-glass before, so she thought the people must have found another sun to replace her and ran from the cave in a rage. The others immediately stretched ropes across the mouth of the cave to stop her from going back into it again, but there was no need. By then she had discovered that it was her own shining face looking back at her. She was delighted by this and by the necklaces, as well as the singing and dancing for, truth to tell, she had begun to feel lonely in her cave. So once more the sun's bright rays lit the earth and the trees and flowers and rice began to grow again in its heat. Then everyone suddenly remembered the cause of all the trouble.

"If Susanoo had stayed out of heaven when his father told him to, this would never have happened!" they shouted angrily, and went off in a body to look for him. When they found him, they cut off his pigtail as punishment and threw him out of heaven by force.

He landed on his back on the banks of the River Hi in western Japan. He had no idea where he was, but suddenly he saw a pair of chopsticks floating down the river.

"Someone must live here," he muttered and set off up river in the direction from which the chopsticks had come.

After a while he saw an old man and an old woman, crying as if their hearts would break, and holding between them a beautiful young girl.

"What's wrong?" Susanoo asked them.

"We had nine daughters," the old man sobbed, "and now we have only this one girl left."

"What happened to the others?" Susanoo asked.

"A terrible dragon came and ate them all, one by one," wept the old woman. "He has eight heads and eight tails and every year for eight years he has come at this time and snatched one of them. Any minute now he will come for our last daughter."

Susanoo looked at the girl and liked what he saw very much.

"If I save her from the dragon, will you let me marry her?" he asked.

"Yes, oh yes!" they both cried.

So Susanoo told them to make saki, which is a Japanese rice drink which looks like water but is stronger than the strongest whiskey. He put some of the drink into eight bowls and built a high fence around them with an opening opposite each bowl. Then he hid himself and waited.

After a while he heard a terrifying roar and saw the dragon coming towards his hiding place. It was a fearsome sight, with the sixteen eyes in its eight heads as red as glowing embers and flames shooting from its eight mouths.

Suddenly it smelled the saki. For a moment its eight tails lashed the ground. Then, one by one, its eight heads found the eight openings in the fence and the eight bowls on the other side of it. Eight tongues began to lap the saki until the eight bowls were dry as a bone. Then, as Susanoo had hoped, the sixteen eyes began to close. As each of the eight heads drooped in a drunken stupor, Susanoo leaped upon them and lopped them off with his sword until the River Hi ran red with their blood. To his surprise, in the middle of the dragon's dead body he found a sword which had wonderful magic powers.

"With this sword," he told the girl and her parents, "I could defeat any dragon in the world, so you need never be afraid again."

Then, amidst great rejoicing, Susanoo married the girl whose life he had saved. He built a beautiful palace on the island of Izumo and there they lived happily for many years. Moreover, from that time on Susanoo stopped moaning and tormenting people and made peace with his sister Amaterasu. Indeed, as a peace offering, he gave her his magic sword and, because it shone like glass, it reflected her face as well as a looking-glass and so she took such good care of it that it can still be seen today in the Temple of Atsuta near the city of Nagoya.

❖

Isis

❖

Egypt

❖

More than three thousand years before the birth of Christ, a baby girl was born in the swamps of the Nile Delta. She was the daughter of Nut, goddess of the sky, and her name was Isis. When still only a child, she was married to Osiris, King of Egypt, and so became a queen long before she would have been old enough for secondary school if she had lived today.

Osiris was the tallest man in Egypt, dark-skinned and handsome, and Isis loved him. He was a good king, teaching his people how to make tools for ploughing and reaping and how to grow grain and grapes to make bread and wine. Isis helped him by teaching the women how to grind corn and spin the flax their men grew, and how to weave the flax to make cloth. She also knew the secrets of the herbs and flowers and berries that cured sickness and these things too she taught to the people.

At night, when Osiris was tired after a day drawing up wise laws, Isis used to sing to him. Then he invented the flute so he could accompany her on it when she sang. After that he also taught the people how to make and play flutes, but what Isis liked best was that he always talked over the affairs of the state with her and listened to her advice about his plans for building new towns or temples. So it was that, when war broke out on Egypt's borders and Osiris had to go away to restore peace, Isis was well able to rule Egypt in his place.

"Do take care," she said to him, as he got ready to leave at the head of his army.

"Don't be afraid," he told her. "I hate all violence and I mean to end the trouble without any killing."

Isis wondered how this was possible, for there had been wars and killing ever since she could remember, but so greatly were even the fiercest of Egypt's enemies impressed by Osiris's kind and gentle manner that soon he returned safely with all his men.

"How did you manage it?" Isis cried in delight, but Osiris only smiled.

"I played them music on my flute and sang to them. After they heard the music they listened to what I had to say and we were able to settle our differences by talking."

There was one man, however, who did not share in the general rejoicing at Osiris's safe return and that was Seth, Osiris's red-headed younger brother. He was jealous of his elder brother's success and of his popularity with the people. Besides, he wanted to be king instead of him and, since Osiris and Isis had not yet had a son, he was next in line for the throne. He thought about this for a long time and worked out an evil plan.

One day a messenger arrived at the royal palace.

"Your brother Seth invites you to a banquet to celebrate your safe return," the messenger told Osiris.

"The queen and I will be glad to accept," Osiris replied.

The messenger looked uneasy.

"Because the banquet is to honour you as commander of the army," he stammered, "it will be a military affair and wives will not be present."

"What?" cried Osiris angrily. "Does my brother insult his queen?"

The messenger threw himself flat on his face on the floor before the king, fearing for his life, but Isis put her hand on the king's arm.

"Don't be angry, my love," she said. "There will probably be a lot of drinking and the men will want to tell rude jokes without having to watch their tongues in front of women. To tell you the truth, long banquets with endless toasts bore me and I'll be glad to stay home and rest. It's been hard work, running the country on my own."

So Osiris went to the banquet by himself. There a feast of many dishes was set before him and Seth's seventy-two other guests. These were all friends of his brother and Osiris thought it a little odd that none of his own friends had been invited, since the banquet was supposed to be in his honour. There was, as Isis had guessed, much drinking of toasts, and then a great wooden casket was carried in by four servants.

It was carved in the shape of a boat, gilded and inlaid with ivory, and everyone cried out at its beauty and richness.

"I'd love to own such a fine work of art," exclaimed one of the guests.

"So would I!" cried another.

"Very well," Seth said. "I will give it to whichever of you is most fitted to have it."

"And how shall our fitness be judged?" asked Osiris.

"He most fitted to own it will be he who best fits into it," Seth laughed.

So, one after another, each of the seventy-two guests climbed into the casket and lay down inside it, but all were too short.

"It looks as if it must have been meant for me," Osiris smiled, "for I must surely be the only man in the country tall enough to stretch from one end to the other."

"Prove it!" challenged the others, so Osiris climbed into the casket.

As he had predicted, it fitted him perfectly but, before he could rise and claim his prize, the others flung themselves upon the casket, slamming the lid shut and nailing it down.

"Now I'm the king!" cried Seth, ordering his servants to throw the casket into the River Nile.

When word reached Isis that her husband had been murdered she was heartbroken, but she did not weep for long.

"Time enough to mourn when I've recovered the king's body," she said.

Meanwhile, the wooden casket had floated down the Nile and out into the Mediterranean Sea. There it drifted north until it was washed up on the coast near Byblos, in what is now Lebanon. Hardly had it come to rest beside a young tamarisk tree then the tree began to grow at the most amazing speed. So fast did it grow that, within a few days, the casket was completely hidden inside its trunk and the tree was so huge that the King of Byblos noticed it.

"That's the very tree I need to hold up the roof of my new summer palace," he cried. "Let it be cut down at once and shaped into a pillar."

No sooner had the tree been cut down, however, then everyone noticed the most beautiful smell coming from it. There was so much talk of this that, in the end, Isis heard of it and, being the daughter of a goddess, knew at once what it meant. She therefore hurried to Byblos where the king, on hearing her story, allowed her to inspect the tree trunk. To his amazement, she pulled out the casket and opened it, revealing the body of Osiris.

Then Isis truly mourned her husband, tearing her robes and cutting off her long black hair, before finally transporting the casket back to Egypt. She meant to build a fine tomb to house it, in which she could put all the king's most prized possessions so that, when he had travelled with the sun through the sky in his boat, he would have them all to enjoy in the next world, for this was the custom. Fearing that Seth might try to prevent her, however, she decided to hide the casket until the tomb was ready. She remembered the swamps of Buto from her childhood in the Nile Delta and thought no one would ever look in such a desolate spot. How was she to know that Seth would choose this very place for a moonlight duck-shoot? So it was that one of Seth's beaters came upon the casket amongst the reeds and told the king.

"I'll make sure Osiris can't lord it over me when I arrive in the next world," Seth swore, and ordered that the body be cut into fourteen separate pieces.

Then, abandoning his hunt, he boarded the royal barge and sailed the length of the Nile, throwing pieces of Osiris's body out as he went. He threw out a leg here and an arm there, sometimes on the east bank and sometimes on the west, until the pieces were scattered throughout the length of the kingdom.

"Now," he laughed, "since only a whole man can travel in the sun's boat, he will never reach the next world."

Nepthys, Seth's wife, disgusted at what her husband had done, slipped out of the palace before he got back and made her way to where Isis sat weeping.

"Let me try to make amends by helping you to find Osiris's body," she said, "for I too am the daughter of a goddess and know magic spells."

So Isis and Nepthys set out to search throughout the land. For many weeks they searched until Nepthys was ready to give up.

"Go home if you wish," Isis told her, "but I will never give up."

"I will never desert you, lady," Nepthys cried

and, the very next day, hidden in the reeds growing along the west bank of the Nile, they found the left leg of Osiris.

"Now," Isis cried in triumph, "I know it's the will of the sun god, Amun Ra, that Osiris shall go with him on his journey through the skies. I'll build a monument here by the riverbank to mark the spot where this leg was found."

No sooner was the monument built, however, then Isis continued the search. As the months went by and they moved further and further up river they found more and more pieces of Osiris's body and, in each place, Isis built a monument. Soon she had found everything but his head. By then, however, they had travelled over two hundred miles through the Arabian Desert and had crossed the border into Upper Egypt.

"The first cataract is only two or three days' journey up river," Nepthys told Isis, "and that would have stopped the royal barge from going any further. Unless we find the head of Osiris soon I'm afraid we must have missed it."

"No," Isis replied, "we found the lower limbs first, so the head will be the last thing Seth threw out."

So they went on until they reached Abydos and there, hidden in a field of growing cotton, Isis found the head of Osiris.

"Thanks be to Amun Ra!" she cried. "Here I will raise the greatest monument of all."

Then, when the final and largest monument was finished, she carried all the pieces of Osiris's body up river as far as Philae. There she laid them all out and, using all her skills, stitched the pieces together again, bandaging the joints after anointing them with sacred oils. When her work was done, Osiris looked as he had done when alive, apart from the whiteness of his face, for no blood coursed through his veins.

"O my beloved," Isis cried, taking his body in her arms, "how I wish you were alive to return my embrace!"

Amun Ra must have heard her for, as she chanted the magic spells she had learned from her mother, Osiris suddenly stirred. Then, to her great joy, he sat up and clasped her in his arms.

"My dearest wife," he said, "your love and loyalty have restored me to life. Now no one can ever harm me again, for the life you have given me is eternal."

"Then you can reclaim your throne," Isis cried.

"If I wished I could," Osiris agreed, "but I would rather leave that task to my son."

"Your son?" gasped Isis. "What son?"

"The son you and I will give life to before I leave you," Osiris told her, "for I must soon return to the other world to rule over the kingdom of the dead."

At the thought of parting with him yet again, Isis began to cry, but Osiris brushed away her tears.

"Do not weep, my love," he said gently, "for soon you will join me there and then our happiness will have no end. In the meantime, you must bring up our son to be as wise a ruler as you proved yourself to be while I was away."

So, after a brief spell of happiness with Isis, Osiris left the earth once more to become king of the next world, giving everlasting life to all the dead who he thought deserved it. Then Isis gave birth to their son Horus, the Hawk-Eyed, bringing him up in the marshes of the Delta in great secrecy, hidden away until he was old enough to avenge his father and regain his throne.

This, after many adventures, he did, ruling the land wisely for many years before following his mother into the next world. There he joined his father in judging the dead, his special task being to weigh each newcomer on a scales with only a feather in the balance, for the hearts of those who have led a good life are lighter than the lightest swans down. But ever after, the ancient Egyptians anointed their dead with sacred oils and bandaged them, just as Isis did with Osiris, which is why their bodies never decayed, but can still be examined by archaeologists today.

❖

The Yellow Emperor and
the Metal Monster

❖

China

❖

A few hundred years later, a monster ravaged the land of China. He had the body of a human but he was horrible to look at for he was not only enormous in size but was made entirely of metal, with six arms, eight fingers on each hand and feet like a bull. He also had four eyes in his head, which was of iron, with hair that stuck up all round it like spears, and two large horns made of bronze. These he would use like a battering ram to attack buildings. Considering his appearance, it was hardly surprising that he had strange tastes in food, living mainly on sand, stones and scraps of metal.

This hideous creature liked nothing better than to fight and used to spend his time travelling backwards and forwards across the country, attacking everything and everyone in his path. Some people said he had the power to be in several places at once, so many thousands had he killed, but others said it was not that he himself was in several places but that he had seventy-two identical brothers. Whichever story was the true one, everyone was agreed that, when he was on the warpath, a comet would appear in the sky overhead and that this moved about with him, just like the banner of an advancing army.

The bravest warriors and the largest armies had failed to defeat this monster, whose name was Ch'i-Yu. Indeed, he seemed to be indestructible for, if anyone actually succeeded in hacking off one of his metal limbs, he was able to make a new one immediately within his own body, inside which fire constantly raged. So, when his banner appeared one day in the sky over the palace of the Yellow Emperor, there was panic among the people, for the emperor was that rarest of creatures: a ruler loved by every one of his subjects.

His name was Shen Yen, but he had been nicknamed the Yellow Emperor (or Pin Yin Huang Ti in Chinese) because of the yellow soil of his kingdom, which was the Kingdom of the Centre, in between the Kingdom of the North Seas and the Kingdom of the South Seas. He was only seven when he became emperor but, instead of playing all day by the pool full of fat carp in the palace garden and leaving the work of running the country to his elderly ministers, Shen Yen began right away planning how to govern his kingdom better.

One night he dreamed of a wonderful country where all the laws were sensible and fair, where people lived in fine wooden houses instead of mud huts and everyone living near a river had strong wooden boats for fishing, everyone living on the plains had wooden carts to take their crops to market and everyone living near a forest had a bow and arrow for hunting. When he woke, Shen Yen started to put into practice everything in his dream until his land was happy and rich. He even taught the people to write, something that until then only emperors could do, so when Ch'i-Yu chose to attack the emperor it was a real disaster.

"Run for your life!" his ministers screamed, as they ran headlong towards the forest, but Shen Yen would not run.

"I shall stay and fight this monster," he cried.

"Don't be foolish, your Imperial Majesty," shouted his courtiers, as they fled after the ministers. "No-one has ever defeated Ch'i-Yu. Look, even your army knows it!"

Then Shen Yen saw to his anger that his great Imperial Army had turned tail and fled to the forest just as fast as his ministers and courtiers. In minutes he was alone in his palace. Knowing that he faced certain death at the metal hands of Ch'i-Yu, he took up his sword with trembling hands. Then he heard a mighty roar. Thinking it must be Ch'i-Yu advancing on the palace, he ran out, only to gasp at the amazing sight in front of him. Coming up the long flight of steps in front of the palace was an army of wild beasts. There were battalions of lions, tigers, leopards, cheetahs and jaguars, followed by whole companies of bears and black panthers.

"Since your own army has deserted you, Shen Yen Huang Ti," the lion general roared, "we have come to fight for you against Ch'i-Yu."

"Then let us not wait here for him," Shen Yen cried, "but go to meet him and surprise him."

So he led his strange army to the plain of Chuo-lu, where they saw the fearsome monster clanking towards them. On seeing them, Ch'i-Yu waved his six metal arms threateningly and rolled on towards them like a giant tank, looking as if he would roll right on over them, crushing their limbs into the mud.

"Spread out and encircle him!" ordered Shen Yen but, as the great beasts melted away to left and right, a strange thing happened. As steam comes for the spout of a boiling kettle, so mist began to rise from the top of Ch'i-Yu's head, until the whole plain was covered in a thick fog. The army of wild beasts could not see their enemy to surround him nor, since he was made of metal, had he a scent they could pick up. As for Shen Yen, now his strange army had been swallowed up by the mist, he felt alone once more. Nor had he any way of telling from which direction Ch'i-Yu might attack him. He strained his ears for any sound that might warn him of the monster's approach. Suddenly he heard a clanking, as of a heavy metal object moving towards him and spun around to face it but no sooner had he done so than he heard a clanking from behind him. He spun round once more only to hear the clanking from all sides. He remembered the stories of how Ch'i-Yu was said to be able to be in several places at once.

Then Shen Yen remembered the invention he had been working on for the past few weeks. He had

had this idea that a magnet might turn to the magnetic north so that, even in a strange forest, or on a starless night, people could always find their way. He had named his invention "the compass" and, although he had not yet got it to work properly, his pouch was full of the many magnets with which he had been experimenting. A magnet would surely swing round to face the metal of Ch'i-Yu's body, he thought.

Quickly setting his largest magnet in place, he watched it as it swung firmly to face his right. The clanking might come from all sides, he thought, but his magnet told him that the metal was in one place only. At that moment he felt hot breath on his hand and, turning, saw the lion general at his side.

"We couldn't find Ch'i-Yu in the fog, Shen Yen Huang Ti," he growled softly, "and there were strange sounds all around us, so I came back for fresh orders, since you at least we could scent."

"Good," said Shen Yen. "I think perhaps Ch'i-Yu has called up demons to help him by making these sounds, so we will believe he is in many places at once. I know of only one thing that will scare away such demons and that is the Winged Dragon. Tell your troops to imitate his cry. Then let them attack the real Ch'i-Yu, who is over somewhere to my right."

The lion general disappeared silently into the mist again and, in a few minutes, the most horrible cries echoed through the darkness. So frightful were they that they made even Shen Yen, who knew what they were, shudder. At once there was a whirring of wings from all around, as if an army of great moths had suddenly taken to the skies, and the clanking stopped.

"Your demons have fled from the Winged Dragon, who fights for me!" Shen Yen cried loudly into the fog to his right. "Now let us see how brave you are, Ch'i-Yu!"

He drew his sword and strode forward in the direction in which his magnet had pointed, but suddenly an even more terrible howl stopped him in his tracks. It was louder than all the other cries put together, making his blood run cold, and it seemed to come from right in front of him. Then there was a deafening metallic crash. As Shen Yen stood there, expecting Ch'i-Yu to fall upon him out of the swirling mist, it suddenly lifted as if blown from beneath by a great wind, and he saw right in front of him the most terrifying sight. The vast metal body of Ch'i-Yu lay stretched on the ground, his great iron head severed from his body and, above him, breathing fire, his snake-like tail lashing the ground, was the Winged Dragon himself.

His head was like that of an angry turkey-cock, though it was as big as an elephant's, and his great wings beat the air, while his eagle-like claws still clung to the torn strips of metal that had once been Ch'i-Yu. Shen Yen trembled at the sight for, though his enemy had been so miraculously defeated, he was even more afraid of the Winged Dragon. Before he could move, however, the Winged Dragon sensed his presence and, letting go of the metal limbs, which fell to the ground with a dull clank, turned to face him.

"You called me up, Shen Yen Huang Ti," he roared, in a voice like the rumble of thunder, "so here I am. The dragon gods are pleased with the way you have ruled your kingdom and with your courage in facing the monster Ch'i-Yu. They have decreed that you shall be victorious over all who ever attempt to destroy your kingdom and it shall grow to include all the tribes of the Yellow River Valley. Then one day you shall be declared immortal, as we are. Now go back to your palace and seek a princess wise and kind enough to rule by your side."

Too astonished to speak, Shen Yen stared as the Winged Dragon rose into the air and flew away until he was no more than a speck in the sky. Then he turned to thank his loyal army of beasts, but they too had disappeared, returning to their forests now he no longer needed them, so he did as the Winged Dragon had ordered.

He found a princess who bred silkworms and wove wonderful rich cloth from their silk and, in time, they married and lived happily in the palace. The new empress taught the art of silk-weaving to their subjects while the emperor found out how to make his compass work and went on to invent many other things too. Above all, he ruled his kingdom in peace and harmony, just as the Winged Dragon had said he would.

❦❦❦

❖

Feridun and
the Serpent King

❖

Persia

❖

Not long after, in the bleak desert of eastern Persia near the border between what are now Iran and Afghanistan, there lived a boy called Zohak who thought only of becoming rich and powerful. Since his father was king of Persia, everything he wished for would probably have become his in time, but Zohak was impatient as well as ambitious.

"My father could easily live another twenty years," he grumbled, "and by then I'll be too old to enjoy my wealth and power."

One day he was wandering around the palace when he found himself beside the kitchens and saw, bending over a great cooking pot, a man he had never seen before.

"Are you new here?" he asked.

"I'm the new chef," the man told him, "and my name is Ahriman."

Now Zohak ought to have known that that was one of the names used by the prince of demons but, if he did, it only made him all the more curious.

"And what is your particular job?" he asked, "among the many chefs we employ in our kitchens?"

"I'm the meat chef," Ahriman told him. "I specialise in cooking the flesh of animals."

For a moment Zohak was shocked. Everyone in the kingdom was vegetarian and for meat dishes to be cooked in the palace was extraordinary. It was against the religious laws and he wondered who could have ordered such dishes. The more he thought about it, however, the more he was fascinated and excited by the idea of tasting meat.

"Do you kill the animals yourself?" he asked.

"With this," Ahriman nodded, picking up a great knife which glittered in the light. "It's so sharp it would kill any animal, however large. In fact, it would even kill a man, whether he be peasant or king. Would you like to hold it in your hand?"

Zohak took the knife and immediately a strange feeling of power surged through him. As if in a dream, he walked straight into his father's study, where the king was examining a parchment and, before his father could even look up from his reading, he plunged the knife through his back and into his heart.

"Now I shall be king," Zohak said, as his father fell dead at his feet.

So Zohak became a rich and powerful ruler while still very young, just as he had wished. He gave a great many banquets and for these Ahriman served the flesh of sheep and goats instead of dishes made from beans and lentils and chick peas. The people were scandalised but Zohak was delighted with the variety and delicacy of the dishes Ahriman cooked and said that he would give his chef anything he asked for in return.

"I ask only one thing, your Majesty," Ahriman replied. "Allow me to kiss your bare shoulders."

It seemed a strange request but Zohak, having expected to have to part with jewellery or gold, thought he had got off lightly. He therefore agreed at once but, no sooner had Ahriman pressed his lips to Zohak's skin than he disappeared in a flash of light. From each of the king's shoulders, in the spot which Ahriman's lips had touched, sprang a black snake, the lower half of their swaying bodies remaining inside Zohak's frame, so that the king had live serpents growing from his two shoulders like two extra arms.

He cried out in horror to the guards, who at once drew their swords and cut off the snakes' bodies above the king's shoulders. Immediately, however, two more grew in their place.

"Get me a doctor!" screamed Zohak in rage and fear. "Let my kingdom be searched high and low for someone who can cure me of this terrible affliction!"

So a proclamation was read in every town and village throughout the land. A few days later a tall, distinguished-looking man, wearing a cloak with strange lettering embroidered on it, arrived at the palace gates.

"My name is Angra Mainyu," he told the guard. "I'm a famous doctor from India and, as I was travelling through your kingdom, I heard your proclamation. If the king wishes I will prescribe a remedy for his unusual complaint."

He was at once brought to the king who, like his courtiers, failed to recognise the demon prince in his new disguise. He pretended to examine Zohak, asking him questions about his health and the behaviour of the snakes. Then he gave his verdict.

"The serpents must be fed daily on human brains," he announced. "After a few months of this diet they will gradually shrivel and die."

Then, with the king's thanks and many gifts, he left the palace as mysteriously as he had appeared. Now Zohak, already made ruthless by his ambition, became a monster. Everyone in the kingdom lived in fear that they or their loved ones would be the next to be seized and murdered, so that their brains might be fed to the serpents. Worse still, the serpents showed no sign of dying in a few months, or even in a few years, but seemed to grow larger and hungrier than ever. Yet Zohak did not abandon the doctor's awful remedy and soon the whole of Persia trembled under Zohak's long reign of terror.

Then one night the king had a nightmare. He dreamed that he was chained to a rocky wall and standing over him was a handsome young nobleman. Next morning he sent for his wisest fortune-tellers, demanding that they interpret his dream. For a long time no one spoke, for they were all afraid. Finally a man called Zirek, who was as honest as he was wise, stepped forward.

"Everyone must die some day," he said, "whether he be king or beggar. Someone must one day inherit your throne and you have dreamed of that man."

Zohak went crazy with terror. He did not have Zirek put to death, as everyone had expected, but he did something worse. Realising that his dream was of the future and the man in it very young, he ordered that every boy born in the kingdom was to be killed, for he hoped in this way to prevent his dream from coming true.

Now a young noblewoman called Firanak had just given birth to a little boy she had called Feridun. When she heard of Zohak's terrible order she snatched her newborn baby from the cradle and ran from her fine house to the cowsheds. There she hid him in the straw, meaning to come back to feed him as soon as she could do so without being seen. Because she was known to have been expecting a baby, however, she was closely watched and so was afraid to go to the stables in case she led Zohak's men to her baby. Fearing the child would die of hunger, she waited anxiously for a chance to slip away unnoticed.

Meanwhile Feridun had woken and begun to cry with hunger. In time his cries would have given him away if a miracle had not taken place. A cow called Purmajeh came over to him and fed him with her own milk, so that he gurgled contentedly and went back to sleep again. Day after day Purmajeh fed the baby in this way until it was safe for Firanak to escape with him into the mountains and across the border to safety. There she brought him up like a nobleman's son, teaching him art, science and the law.

One day a man appeared at Zohak's palace,

where the king was seated on his balcony, giving judgement on cases brought before him by the people standing on the steps below.

"I'm Kaweh the Smith," the man cried, "and I demand justice!"

"Who has wronged you?" asked the king.

"You have!" shouted the smith, "for you have killed all my sons, one after the other, to feed your serpents."

Then, before the king could have him arrested, he ran from the palace into the crowds milling around the entrance to the bazaar.

"He speaks truly!" cried one of the men who had heard what he said.

"Our sons too have been killed!" agreed another, while a third cried:

"This king doesn't give justice, only cruelty!"

Soon the whole crowd had taken up the cry for justice and revenge. Then the smith seized a lance from the hand of an astonished guard, powerless to act against so large a mob, tied his smith's apron to the end of it to make a banner and led the crowd of angry men off into the desert, shouting, "We will seek help to save our country from this monster of a king!"

After a while the little army reached the mountains, crossed the border and marched on until they came to the castle where Feridun was living. He saw the men coming towards him from a long way off, because of the cloud of dust raised by their marching feet, and he went out to meet them.

"What can have turned skilled craftsmen and

labourers alike into an army?" he asked. "And what brings you here?"

Kaweh the Smith told him what had happened. Then Feridun snatched up a great club, which only a man of unusual strength could have raised from the ground.

"My mother has told me of this evil king, who has also wronged my mother and me," he cried. "Now I will lead your army against him!"

So, mounting his horse, he led the little band of smiths and carpenters, weavers and carpetmakers, artists and labourers, through the winding passes back over the border and across the desert until they arrived back at Zohak's palace. When they arrived, the king was out hunting and no one dared to oppose the army of determined men who forced their way into the palace. Inside, in a locked inner room, Feridun found the most beautiful girl he had ever seen. She had skin like a rose petal and eyes as black as sloes.

"Who are you?" Feridun asked, staring at her in wonder.

"I'm Princess Shehrinaz, daughter of King Jemshid," she told him, in a voice that reminded him of the singing of nightingales. "Ever since Zohak defeated my father in battle and sawed his body in two he has held me prisoner here."

"You are a prisoner no longer," Feridun told her, "and as soon as I have dealt with Zohak I will take you to wherever you wish to go."

Shehrinaz looked at her handsome rescuer and smiled.

"I ask only to go wherever you go," she said.

Meanwhile a servant had brought Zohak news of Feridun's arrival. At once he put on a magic suit of armour which made him invisible and set out for the palace. The first thing he saw when he arrived was Feridun, seated in his chair of state with Shehrinaz at his side, looking at him adoringly. This so enraged Zohak that he forgot he was invisible.

"I'll teach you to usurp my throne!" he roared, drawing his sword and rushing at Feridun.

Though Feridun could not see him, he immediately swung his great club and brought it down on the spot from which the words had come. At once the sound of splintering armour told him that he had struck home and, as the broken armour fell away, they could all see Zohak lying unconscious on the ground.

"Kill him! Kill him!" everyone cried but Shehrinaz laid her small white hand on his arm.

"No," she said, "that would be too easy a death after all the suffering he has caused. Make him your prisoner, as he made me."

So Feridun chained Zohak to the wall of a cave in the side of Mount Demarand, just as Zohak had foreseen in his nightmare. Then, with Shehrinaz always at his side, he became king in Zohak's place, setting to rights all the wrongs of that terrible reign and ruling the people with wisdom and justice for five hundred years.

❧❧❧

❖

Rama and
the Ten-Headed Giant

❖

India

❖

Round about the same time there lived in India a king who had three wives. The son of his first wife was called Rama, the son of his second wife Bharata and the son of his third wife Lakshmana. The three boys all grew up strong and brave, but Rama and Lakshmana did everything together, so that Bharata often felt left out. Even when Rama married Sita, the beautiful daughter of a neighbouring king, Lakshmana still spent most of his time with the young couple so that Bharata felt more left out than ever and his mother grew jealous for him.

She grew even more jealous when the king, deciding that he was too old to go on ruling the kingdom, announced that Rama was to be crowned king in his place.

"You should force the king to make your son his heir," her lady-in-waiting suggested.

"How could I do that?" the king's second wife asked.

"When the king comes to you this evening," her

lady-in-waiting said, "pretend to be sick with grief."

So, when the king arrived he found his second wife writhing about on the floor as if in agony.

"What's wrong?" the king cried. "Is someone tormenting you? Just name him and he shall be punished!"

But the queen said nothing, just as her lady-in-waiting had advised. Only when the king, by then really alarmed, swore to do anything in his power to make her better did she speak. Calling all the gods to witness his promise, she demanded that Rama be exiled to the forest of Dandaka and her son Bharata crowned king in his place. The king raged and pleaded, for he loved Rama dearly, but his wife insisted.

To everyone's surprise, when Rama was told of the change of plan, he refused to fight Bharata for the crown.

"Let it be as my father wishes," he said, and went to say goodbye to his mother, but Lakshmana's face turned red with anger.

"If Rama must go into exile I will go too," he cried, "for he has been unfairly treated."

Sita, too, insisted on going with her husband, despite the dangers and discomforts he pictured for her.

"I fear lions, tigers and snakes less than I fear living without you," she cried. "I will happily live on roots and berries if I may be by your side."

So the three young people were driven by chariot to the forest. There, by a sandy river bank, Lakshmana built a little cottage with mud walls and a thatched roof, where they lived happily amongst the trees, creepers and blue water-lilies.

Now there was a giant called Ravana living in Sri Lanka with twenty arms and ten heads, each topped by a jewel-encrusted crown, for Ravana was king of an evil race called the Rakshasas. When he heard that Rama, Lakshmana and Sita were living in the forest and that Sita was strikingly beautiful, he determined to make her his third wife, so he turned one of his servants into a beautiful golden deer and ordered him to go to Sita. She was gathering flowers in the forest when she saw the magic deer, nibbling leaves from a tree.

"Rama," she called softly, "come quickly and capture this deer for me. He's the most beautiful creature I've ever seen and I'd love him for a pet!"

So Rama and Lakshmana, holding a net between them, crept towards the deer. Again and again it let them get close and then bounded away, leading them deeper and deeper into the forest and further and further away from Sita. Then Ravana, disguised as a beggar, went to the cottage, asking for food. When Sita brought him fruit, however, he seized her and dragged her to his chariot, hidden amongst the trees. The second he had climbed aboard, with the struggling Sita in his arms, the chariot rose into the air and flew off towards Sri Lanka.

Though Rama was too far away to hear Sita's despairing cries, they did not go unheard. Jatayu, the aged king of the eagles and a son of the god of dawn heard her, and at once flew to try to rescue her, tearing at Ravana with his talons. Each time he succeeded in breaking one of the arms that held Sita prisoner, however, another of the twenty took its place, while his other arms struck with their swords at the eagle's wings until he fell to the ground, mortally wounded. Then Sita, weeping for the brave bird, was carried through the skies to Ravana's island fortress.

Meanwhile, Rama and Lakshmana, having failed to capture the deer, returned to the cottage and discovered Sita was missing. Frantically they searched for her until they came upon the dying eagle, who told them with his last breath what had happened. At once the brothers set off through the forest in pursuit of the chariot. After a while they began to feel that they were being watched, though they could see no one. Then the sound of a bending branch made them look up and there, watching them closely, was a large monkey.

"Why are you following us?" Rama asked him.

"I'm Hanuman, son of the wind," he replied. "I'm also chief minister to the king of the monkeys, who wishes to know what you are doing in his kingdom."

Rama then told him his name and how he was on his way to try to rescue his wife from the ten-headed giant.

"That will be difficult," Hanuman told him. "Miles of sea separate the island of Sri Lanka from India and the king's fortress has walls ten times the height of a man. It's defended by thousands of soldiers, while the king himself has magical powers, so no man can kill him. Nevertheless, your noble deed in giving up your crown is admired in our land and I believe our king will be glad to place his army at your service. No wall is too high for a monkey to climb."

"That would be friendship indeed," cried Rama, "but first I must find Sita and decide how best to rescue her."

"If the king permits, I will undertake this myself," Hanuman told him, so the three of them went straight to the monkey king's palace.

"You shall stay here while Hanuman goes to Sri Lanka," the king said, when they had told their story. "Now I will send for my army."

Hardly had Rama finished thanking him before the troops began to arrive. From the distant forests, mountains and shores came millions of monkeys. There were large and small monkeys, grey, black and brown monkeys, ones with long curling tails and ones with no more than stumps. When the vast army was camped around the palace, the king ordered Hanuman to set out.

"Take this," Rama said, pulling the signet ring from his finger and giving it to Hanuman. "It will prove to Sita that you come from me."

Then, like ants from an anthill, the monkey army streamed out of the camp, with Hanuman at their head, until they disappeared from sight. After travelling through the forest for days, the army came to a desert. Knowing they would find no food or water there, they gathered berries at the forest edge but, by the third day, these were all gone and still the desert seemed to stretch far ahead of them. By nightfall they were faint with hunger and thirst. Seeing them coming, Sampati, king of the vultures, was happy. So old that all the feathers had gone from his wings, he could no longer fly in search of prey.

"All these monkeys are going to die at my feet," he croaked. "I'll be able to feed on them for the rest of my days!"

When Hanuman saw him, however, he cried out to him, "We bring sad news, O king of the vultures. Your brother Jatayu, king of the eagles is dead!"

Then Sampati wept as Hanuman told him how Jatayu had died, trying to rescue Sita, for whom they were now searching.

"It was foretold," the great bird answered, "that if ever I helped Rama my wings would have new life, so now I'll tell you that, beyond these hills, is an oasis fringed with date palms."

At once new young feathers began sprouting on Sampati's wings and the great bird spread them, rising into the air.

"Follow me," he cried, "and I will lead you there."

While the starving monkeys ate and drank their fill, Sampati flew across the sea to Sri Lanka until he was over Ravana's fortress. There he soon found Sita, sitting sadly in a lovely garden full of fruit, flowers and birds, but it was surrounded by Rakshasi giants, guarding her. Returning, he told all this to Hanuman.

"I must go to her," Hanuman cried, and he and his monkey army followed Sampati's directions and soon reached the shore. There they looked in dismay at the great stretch of sea between them and the island of Sri Lanka.

"It must be bridged," Hanuman ordered. "Every monkey must bring rocks and trees until a causeway runs across to the island, but first I will jump the gap and tell Sita that help is at hand."

"No monkey could jump so far!" they cried, but Hanuman climbed to the top of Mahandra Hill and, using all his powers, made himself twice his normal size. Then, praying for strength, he held his breath, folded back his ears, stiffened his muscles till his hair stood on end and pressed down on his paws. Water spurted from the hole he tore in the ground as he rose with a roar into the sky like a comet, casting a shadow like that of a great ship on to the sea beneath him. When he saw the coastline of Sri Lanka and Ravana's fortress below him, he dropped down and landed on top of Mount Suvala.

Reducing himself to normal size again, Hanuman quickly scaled the fortress walls, ran along the top of them until he saw the garden the vulture had described and then leaped into the branches of a mango tree. Beneath it, her face wet with tears, sat the most beautiful woman he had ever seen and Hanuman knew then that he had indeed found the princess.

"Take heart," he called softly down through the branches. "Rama is coming to rescue you."

Sita looked up but, seeing only a monkey, feared

it was a trick of Ravana's. Then Hanuman dropped Rama's ring into her lap.

"Here's proof that I come from Rama," he whispered.

Weeping for joy, Sita handed him a sparkling jewel.

"Take this to him in return," she said. "It has not left my forehead since his father placed it there at our wedding."

Saying goodbye to her, Hanuman took the jewel and quickly sprang from the mango tree to the top of the fortress wall. As he ran along it, he suddenly saw, parked beside a clump of trees, Ravana's aerial chariot and, swinging by his tail, dropped into it. Before the startled guards knew what was happening, it rose into the air and flew straight to the palace of the monkey king, where Hanuman told Rama the good news.

Clutching the jewel Sita had sent him, Rama poured out his thanks to Hanuman and then, without pausing to eat, he and Lakshmana leaped into the chariot at his side.

"Let us fly straight to Sita," he cried, "without waiting for the army, except for the few warriors we can fit into the chariot with us!"

"We will not succeed without the army," Hanuman told him, "but we will not have to wait for long, as you will see if you look down."

Then Rama saw below the causeway of stones and tree trunks stretching most of the way across to the island.

"Oh Hanuman," Rama cried, "wisest and most

daring of monkeys, who else could have planned so great a bridge! The moment it's finished we'll attack!"

But Ravana's scouts had seen the monkeys' work and told Ravana.

"Call up the army!" Ravana ordered. "Let every man sharpen his arrows or his axe and be ready to attack, for only Rama could cause a road to travel across the sea!"

So an army of giants was gathered, facing the shore, ready to advance the minute that the road reached land.

"Let my chariot be brought!" Ravana ordered then, "so I may fly over this strange road and see how big an army Rama has collected."

Only then did his charioteer learn that the chariot was missing, for the guards had been afraid to report it in case Ravana killed them in rage. Meanwhile, Rama had become too impatient to wait for the bridge to be finished.

"Let half-a-dozen of your best men come with Lakshmana and me in the chariot," he told Hanuman. "We will try to rescue Sita while you and your army attack from the shore."

"Very well," Hanuman agreed, "but I will order the attack now, for my army can jump the stretch of sea that remains unbridged. That way we may surprise Ravana."

So it was that, before Ravana could order his troops to advance, monkeys began to hurtle down upon Mount Suvela.

"It's raining monkeys!" cried the startled guards.

As the monkeys attacked fiercely, Ravana's army was hastily turned around to face this new direction and a terrible battle began. Hearing the sound of fighting, Sita thrilled to the thought that Rama must be near, but suddenly she saw Ravana's chariot overhead. Fearing that Ravana was coming for her she turned to run, only to hear Rama's voice, calling her name. Her delight was short-lived, however, as the palace guards rushed upon them. Rama and Lakshmana drew their swords, as did the monkey soliders with them and, though there were three guards to every one on Rama's side, so bravely did Rama and Lakshmana fight that soon they were all dead, dying or fleeing.

"Take Sita to safety in the chariot," Rama ordered the monkey captain, "for we must help Hanuman."

Sita did not want to leave Rama, but she dared not disobey him. Meanwhile, news had reached Ravana that the money army was winning.

"Then I will kill Sita," he cried. "She has caused all this trouble. When she's dead Hanuman will have no one to rescue and will withdraw his army."

His horrified ministers tried to dissuade him but, with two of his trusted officers, Ravana set out for his fortress. So it was that Rama and Lakshmana met him, face-to-face, outside the walls. Single-handed, Lakshmana fought both officers as Rama advanced on Ravana. Like two lions they attacked each other and Rama managed to cut off one of Ravana's ten heads. Immediately, however, another grew in its place. Head after head Rama struck off, but each time other heads grew. Then Rama remembered Hanuman telling him that no man could ever kill Ravana.

"Then let us see what the spear of a god may do," he cried seizing the spear that had been given to him by Vayu, god of death.

Heavy as a mountain, with a point made out of sunlight and fire, the spear smoked as Rama plunged it into Ravana's heart. At once the giant fell to the ground, dead. So his evil reign ended and, after thanking Hanuman and the monkey king, Rama, Sita and Lakshmana returned to their forest home.

When word of the great victory reached the capital there was great rejoicing, especially by Bharata, who loved his brothers and had always been unhappy about what his mother had done.

"It's clear that the gods wish Rama to rule," he cried.

So a great procession set out for the forest and the exiles were brought home. Then Rama was crowned king and ruled with wisdom for many years, his faithful wife Sita and loyal brother Lakshmana always at his side.

❦❦❦

❖

The Giant Lizard and
the Black Snake

❖

Australia

❖

O f course everyone knows how once upon a time huge dinosaurs and enormous elephant-like creatures called mammoths roamed the earth. Not everyone knows, however, that *all* the animals, reptiles and birds were once a great deal bigger than they are today.

Even today in Australia there are lizard-like creatures called iguanas which are as much as five feet long, but once upon a time they were bigger than the biggest crocodiles and liked nothing better for their tea than the flesh of a man or a woman. Worse still, they had poisonous fangs like many snakes have today, though the peculiar thing is that in those days snakes were not poisonous at all and a bite from one of them did no more harm than a bite from a guinea pig. Too many people were being killed by iguanas, however, and one day a meeting was called at the water-hole to try to think of a way to protect people from these terrible giant lizards.

"If anyone has a plan that will rid us of this

threat, let him or her stand up and tell it," the chief said, when everyone had assembled.

The people all looked at each other hopefully, but no one spoke. There was a long, long silence. Then Ooyu-bu-lui, the black snake, rustled into the clearing.

"What's wrong with the humans?" he asked Dinewan, the emu, for he had never known people to sit in silence for so long.

Dinewan explained how the people were all afraid of Mungoon-gali, the iguana.

"And," added Bohra, the giant kangaroo, "even though I'm as big and as strong as Mungoon-gali, I'd be afraid to fight him when one bite of his poisonous fangs would be enough to kill me!"

"I'm not afraid of him," boasted Ooyu-bu-lui. "Just leave it to me and I'll soon deal with him!"

"How?" chorused Dinewan and Bohra.

"Aha, that's my secret!" laughed Ooyu-bu-lui, "but I promise you that, before many days have passed, I'll have taken Mungoon-gali's poison sack away from him."

"You're crazy!" Dinewan told him. "Before you can attack him, he'll bite and kill you."

"That's just where you're wrong," Ooyu-bu-lui retorted. "The trouble with your sort is that you can think of nothing but fighting. I'm going to use cunning, not force."

Leaving them staring after him, Ooyu-bu-lui slid silently away from the water-hole into the bush. A few days went by but nothing happened.

"I knew Ooyu-bu-lui couldn't do anything about Mungoon-gali," the emu told the kangaroo. "He was only boasting."

But the black snake had meant what he said. He waited until Mungoon-gali had eaten a particularly large meal and was lying down to sleep in the sun. Then, even though he knew the giant iguana was feeling lazy and in no humour for attacking anyone, he approached him cautiously, speaking to him from a safe distance.

"Mungoon-gali," he called softly. "I've come as a friend to warn you that the humans are plotting against you."

"Pooh!" scoffed the iguana. "What can they do against me? I've already killed hundreds of them and if any of them come near me I'll kill a lot more."

"You might not be so sure of yourself if you knew their plan," Ooyu-bu-lui told him.

"Then tell me what it is," snarled the iguana. "Quick, or I'll make short work of you too!"

"How can I be sure you won't do that anyway?" asked Ooyu-bu-lui. "You might wait until I came over to whisper their plan to you and then bite me."

"If you tell me their plan, I promise I'll never bite a snake again," Mungoon-gali replied. "Isn't that enough for you?"

"Provided you keep your word," Ooyu-bu-lui said. "But how do I know I can trust you?"

"I'll prove it to you," Mungoon-gali said. "Ask for whatever proof you like."

"Then while I tell you what the tribes planned at

their meeting by the water-hole, let me hold your poison sack," Ooyu-bu-lui told him. "But of course it's up to you. If you don't want to give it to me you'll just have to find out about the plot the hard way."

And the black snake wriggled around as if he was about to slide away into the bush again.

"Wait!" cried Mungoon-gali. "I must know what the tribes have planned."

"Then give me the poison sack," the black snake insisted.

"Wouldn't it do if I just put the sack down on the ground beside me?" Mungoon-gali pleaded, but the black snake shook his head slowly from side to side.

"It would be too easy for you to snatch it up again," he said.

So Mungoon-gali reached into his mouth, drew out the poison sack and pushed it across the clearing to Ooyu-bu-lui.

"Now, quickly, tell me the plot," he cried.

"Certainly," replied Ooyu-bu-lui, popping the poison sack into his own mouth. "It was to trick you into parting with your poison sack!"

Then he slid away as fast as he could through the long grass, leaving the giant lizard staring after him, open-mouthed and furious. And since that day, it is the cunning snakes who have the poison fangs and not the poor stupid iguanas who, even though they are still a lot bigger than lizards, are just as harmless. But though Ooyu-bu-lui tricked Mungoon-gali into giving him his poison sack, he never got from him the secret of the cure for the poison. So it is that the bite of a snake can never harm an iguana, who alone knows which plant to eat to cure a snake bite and is therefore never afraid to attack a snake, unlike other creatures. Indeed, an iguana will never see a snake without attacking him, for he will never forget or forgive the dirty trick the cunning black snake played on him long ago when the world was new.

❖

Sedna

❖

Canada

❖

A very long time ago in Greenland there lived a beautiful girl called Sedna. She was an Inuit, which neighbouring tribes called Eskimo, meaning "those who eat their food raw." Her mother was dead and she had neither brothers nor sisters, but lived all alone with her father beside the sea.

Because she was so beautiful many men wished to marry her. Not only young men from her own tribe but even those from far distant lands called on her, bringing presents and asking her to be their wife, but Sedna would have none of them.

"What's wrong with him?" her father would ask, each time she sent another suitor away in despair.

"Nothing, father," she would answer, "but I've no wish to be married. I'm happy living here with you in our igloo."

Then one day, just as the winter ice was melting in the spring sunshine, a strange kayak appeared in the bay. In it was a handsome young hunter, wearing splendid furs and carrying an ivory spear. He paddled close to the shore but, instead of landing, called to Sedna across the waves that rocked the canoe in which he sat.

"Come, Sedna," he called, as she stood staring at him from the doorway of the igloo. "Only come with me and you shall have necklaces of ivory and fine combs for your hair, carved from the horns of reindeer."

His voice was musical and strange, not unlike the haunting cry of a seabird, and Sedna felt curious. She moved closer to the shore to see him more clearly. There was no doubt that he was the most handsome man she had ever seen.

"Who are you and where do you come from?" she asked.

"I come from the Land of Birds, where there is no hunger," he called softly back to her, "where there is always enough oil for the lamps and meat for the cooking pots. Only come with me and you will never again need to load a frozen dog-sledge or break holes in the ice to fish, but will lie on thick white polar bear skins, warm and content."

Almost as if under a spell, Sedna climbed into his kayak and allowed the stranger to paddle it far away from the shore and her father's home. Not even when her father, returning from hunting caribou, saw her figure disappearing out to sea and cried to her to come back, did she take her eyes from the handsome stranger paddling the canoe.

In alarm her father hurried to where his own

kayak lay on the shore and began hauling it down to the water's edge. By the time he had launched it and fetched the paddle, however, the stranger's kayak with Sedna in the stern had disappeared out of sight. Nevertheless he began to paddle out to sea as hard as he could towards the spot where it had been when he last saw it.

Meanwhile Sedna, still in a trance, had landed on a distant island. Majestic white cliffs rose on all sides, giving the land an air of mystery quite unlike the flat lands of her own ice-bound home.

"Where do you live?" she asked in wonder for, no matter which way she looked, she could see no igloo.

"Over there," he said, pointing to a distant cliff.

He beached the kayak and led Sedna towards the white walls which towered ahead of them, but still she could see no dwelling place, only holes high in the cliff face, in and out of which large seabirds were flying.

"Where?" she asked again.

"Up there! Up there!" he cried, his voice seeming to float away from her on the wind.

Startled, she turned and saw that, where he had been standing, a giant seabird was slowly rising up into the air. Its great wings beat strongly, lifting it high on the wind. It circled high above her head and then flew straight into one of the great jagged holes in the cliff. Then Sedna knew that it was no man she had pledged herself to marry but a spirit, who could assume the shape of a man or bird as he pleased.

Alone and sobbing on that lonely island where no humans had their home, she had little choice but to allow her bird-man, on his return, to carry her on his back up to the cave which was to be her new home.

Next evening he told her that he had to go away for a while. Weeping, she begged him not to leave her captive in the cave for hours by herself, for there was no way she could climb down the sheer cliff-face. He therefore set her down at the foot of the cliff to gather seashells before flying away across the water.

So it was that Sedna's father saw her as he paddled past island after island in search of her. Overjoyed at finding her, he caught her up in his arms. Realising from her sobs of relief that she was as eager to return home as he was to have her back, he asked no questions until he had carried her to his kayak and set out for the open sea once more. As he paddled she told him her strange story.

"And I'm afraid my husband will never let me go," she sobbed, "for he seems to love me very much even though he is not of this world."

"Leave him to me!" her father said confidently, but he had hardly spoken before they both heard shouts from behind them.

"Come back! Come back!" echoed the words over the water, like the lonely cry of a gull.

Then Sedna saw a kayak moving swiftly over the water towards them.

"Quick, hide under those furs!" her father cried, paddling harder than ever in an attempt to shake off their pursuer.

But his efforts were in vain. The spirit, though now in human form, seemed to have strength that was more than human and soon his kayak had almost overtaken theirs.

"Let me see Sedna," he pleaded. "I beg you, let me see my wife!"

But Sedna's father ignored him, redoubling his efforts until his desperate paddling had put a little distance between the two boats once more. This time the sound they heard was unmistakably the harsh cry of a gull and the father looked up to see great wings beating overhead. For a moment he was afraid that the giant bird meant to dive down upon them but then, with a great cry of despair, the creature disappeared into the gathering darkness.

"It's all right," he cried. "He's gone. You can come out now."

Laughing and crying with relief, Sedna struggled out from under the pile of furs at the bottom of the boat, thinking she was safe, but immediately there was a loud clap of thunder directly overhead and lightning zig-zagged the darkening sky. A hundred seabirds seemed to be crying out from all around them and fierce waves buffeted the boat.

"The gods are angry!" Sedna's father cried. "They mean to punish me for helping you to break your marriage vows!"

"We must get back to the land," Sedna urged, seizing a second paddle to help her father in his desperate bid to escape from the raging seas, but it was a hopeless task. Soon it seemed as if the boat would overturn at any moment.

Now words could be heard in the thunder of the waves which tore at the skin of the frail kayak, as if to rip it from the wooden frame over which it was stretched.

"Give us Sedna!" they thundered. "Give us Sedna or we'll drag both of you down together!"

"The gods have spoken," the terrified man gasped, "and I must obey them!"

So he seized his daughter and hurled her overboard into the icy waters. At once she sank beneath the waves but, after a second, her pale face rose to the surface once more as her fingers clutched the side of the boat.

"Cut her free! Cut her free!" thundered the waves.

Half crazy with fear, her father seized an ivory axe and chopped off the clutching fingers. At once the smallest fingers became seals, the thumbs walruses and the biggest fingers whales, as Sedna sank once more beneath the waves. This time she did not rise again and at once the sea grew calm. The thunder and lightning ceased, the sky brightened and the boat began to drift towards the shore even before the shocked man could pick up his paddle again. Hardly knowing what he was doing, he stumbled into his igloo and fell into a deep sleep.

From that day onward, however, he was a changed man. He spoke to no one and he grew thin and gaunt, for he no longer bothered to hunt for food.

"I should have let the gods take me too," he cried aloud one day, "for I would rather be with Sedna at the bottom of the sea than to have to live on with the memory of that awful day!"

That night the tide rose higher than it had ever done before, until it covered the igloo and everything about it, sweeping them all away as if they had never been. So the father was united with Sedna in the kingdom below the waves, where she now rules as goddess of the sea and of all the creatures that live beneath it.

❖

The Fish that Maui Caught

❖

New Zealand

❖

I n a very much warmer part of the world, near a volcano on an island in the middle of the Pacific Ocean, there once lived a Polynesian boy called Maui. He had one brown eye and one green one, and he was left-handed. He was both brave and clever, but he was always getting into trouble because he had no respect for anyone or anything.

Sometimes people said that this was because he was not a human child at all, but had come out of the sea. This was partly true, for he *had* been washed up by the sea, but only because his human mother had thrown him into it soon after he was born because she thought he was dead. Nor was she to be blamed for this, for he neither cried nor moved and was no bigger than a kitten. So she cut off her long hair, wrapped the baby's body in it and floated him away on the tide. Luckily he was found by some sea sprites, who cared for him until he was big and strong, when they set him in the waves near the water's edge to be washed safely back on to the beach again.

Of course his mother was overjoyed to have her youngest son brought back to her alive and well but, though he soon grew to be as tall as his four older brothers, that was the only thing he had in common with them. While they did as they were told and behaved just like everyone else, no one ever knew what Maui would say or do next. One day, for instance, he happened to overhear his mother complaining that the sun moved too fast through the sky.

"I've so much cooking and washing and cleaning to do," she said, "and the sun sets before I have it half-done."

Maui never said a word, but went away and made some strong ropes from the fibre of coconut leaves. Then he climbed up to the crater of the volcano and hid behind a rock. As each sun ray crept up the side of the mountain to touch the edge of the crater, Maui tied it to a tree with one of his ropes until every ray was held fast and the sun was unable to move any further.

"What d'you think you're doing, you stupid boy?" the sun roared at him, burning Maui with all his great heat, so that his skin grew red and blistered and the grass around him turned black.

"If I let you go," shouted Maui, "will you promise to take longer to cross the sky each day, so my mother has time to do all her work before nightfall?"

"Oh, very well," grumbled the sun. "I promise."

So Maui untied the ropes as quickly as he could for, truth to tell, he could not have stood the heat for very much longer.

His mother was very pleased to have a longer day, but she was shocked that her youngest son should have treated the sun so impudently. But then he was always doing outrageous things and his pranks drove his older brothers crazy.

One evening he had been particularly annoying so, next morning, his brothers got up very early and crept out of the house without telling him. A fishing trip had been planned, but they thought it would be a good deal more peaceful, and probably a lot safer too, if their youngest brother was not there tricking about in the boat.

"He'll be awfully angry when he wakes up!" said the brother next in age to Maui.

"I'd like to see his face when he finds we've gone without him!" laughed the third.

"Serves him right!" remarked the second.

"Maybe it will teach him to behave himself in future!" added the eldest, as they paddled out to their favourite fishing ground.

They were about to stow away their paddles and cast out their fishing lines when they were startled to hear a voice from beneath their feet.

"Paddle further out!" it ordered.

The brothers looked at one another in alarm.

"Who said that?" asked the fourth brother nervously.

"The voice seemed to come from right under the boat!" gasped the third.

"From the very depths of the sea!" cried the second.

"It could only be the voice of Tangaroa, god of the ocean!" stammered the eldest.

"No, it's not!" laughed the voice from beneath their feet.

Then the pile of nets and fishing lines at the bottom of the canoe stirred and out from underneath them crawled Maui, grinning from ear to ear.

"Scared you, didn't I?" he chuckled. "That's what you get for trying to slip out without me! I heard you whispering together about your plan so I decided to get to the boat before you. Now, paddle further out!"

"We don't take orders from you!" snapped the eldest.

"Certainly not," agreed the second brother. "You're the youngest so keep quiet and do as you're told!"

"We've always found these fishing grounds good," added the third.

"So this is where we'll cast our lines," cried the fourth.

Maui laughed wickedly.

"Are you sure?" he asked. "Take another look!"

When the brothers looked around them they cried out in surprise for, instead of being close to the rocks near the harbour mouth, they were surrounded by open sea.

"Wherever are we?" cried the fourth brother.

"There's no land in sight!" shouted the third.

"But we're only just outside the bay!" gasped the second.

"This is another of your tricks!" snapped the eldest, glaring at Maui. "What have you done now?"

"My friends the sea sprites took us out on the waves while you were arguing," Maui grinned. "Now they've brought us to *my* fishing grounds, where the biggest fish of all can be caught."

So his older brothers baited their hooks, threw in their lines and caught one fat fish after another. When the boat was full of fish they wanted to head for home, but Maui asked them to wait.

"Now it's *my* turn," he said.

Then he took his own special hook, which he had got from the far end of the world. Made from the jaw bone of a woman who had had magical powers, the hook was itself magic and this Maui tied to the end of his line and baited it.

"Now I'll catch a bigger fish than you have ever seen," he boasted, as he swung his line in a great arc and cast it far out into the blue waters.

Almost at once he felt a weight on the line.

"Come and help me to land my catch," he cried to his brothers, "for it's far too heavy for me to haul in by myself."

So his four brothers joined him in hauling in the line. After they had panted and tugged and heaved for a long time, the largest fish they had ever seen broke the surface of the water. It was miles and miles long and, as they strained and heaved, they found they were hauling the canoe alongside the fish instead of the other way round. Maui bent down and tore the hook from its mouth and, as he did so, the fish became solid land.

"This shall be called Hawaii," said Maui, as his brothers watched him in amazement. "Now paddle a little to the north-west."

Too stunned to argue, his brothers did as he had told them. Once again Maui threw out his line with the magic fish hook on the end and, once again, the hook had hardly sunk below the surface of the water when the line became taut. Tug after tug set the line bobbing in the water and yet again Maui had to call his brothers to help him to haul it in. This time, however, it was not a huge fish but a whole shoal of little fishes that were strung out along the hook of the magic jawbone like beads on a necklace.

There were so many of them that, small though they were, together they were even heavier than the first fish and again the brothers had to heave and strain on the line to pull them alongside—or rather, to pull the canoe over to them. This time, as Maui bent down to unhook them, the fish tried to escape, darting away from the side of the canoe in a curved line, but escape from the magic was impossible. Soon there was a string of small islands running north-west from the big island.

"What are all these to be called?" Maui's eldest brother asked in wonder, but Maui only shrugged his shoulders.

"There are far too many of them to name each one separately," he replied carelessly. "I'm calling them all the Hawaiian Islands. When Tane, god of life and growth, has covered them with trees and creepers, they can be given names by people who come to live on them, so long as one of them is called after me."

Then Maui went on to catch the islands of Samoa and Tonga and Marquesa and Tahiti and Easter Island and the Cook and Tuamotu Islands, which is why there are so many beautiful little islands dotted about in the middle of the great Pacific Ocean. Even the great North Island of New Zealand is called Maui's Fish in the Maori language, with the bay of Wellington thought to be the fish's eye, while the South Island is called Maui's Canoe, with the funny looking hook-shaped Stewart Island which hangs just below it thought to be its anchor. The only island called after Maui himself, however, is among the first he caught, far away to the north amongst the Hawaiian Islands.

❖

How the Llamas and
Parrots Saved the Humans

❖

South America

❖

I t is said that, long after that, the whole world was nearly destroyed and there might not have been a single human being left alive in it had it not been for the llamas. Their shepherd, a member of the Canarian tribe who lived on the lower slopes to the east of the great mountain range that runs up through Peru and into Ecuador, noticed that they had stopped grazing and kept looking up at the sky with big mournful eyes.

"What's wrong with you?" the shepherd asked. "There's good grass on this slope and yet you won't eat."

"It's no good eating," the first llama bleated, "when soon we and all belonging to us will be dead."

"Why do you say that?" the shepherd asked, puzzled. "I see no sign of an enemy coming up from the forests to attack us."

"The danger isn't coming from man," the second llama replied, "but from Viracocha, the Maker of All Things, who is angry at the ways of man. In five days' time the rains will come in great torrents. They will go on until the sea has risen and covered the whole earth and everything on it has been destroyed."

"And is there no escape for us?" cried the shepherd. "Must I and my wife and two sons be drowned?"

"You will," the first llama told him, "unless you collect your wife and family and enough food to last for sixty days and follow me."

So the shepherd and his wife and sons threw blankets over the backs of the two llamas and loaded on to them all the food that they could find. Then they tied ropes around the llamas' necks and let them lead the way up the slopes of the highest mountain in the neighbourhood, which was called Villa-Coto. As they reached the shoulder of the mountain, they heard strange cries coming from the mountain peak.

"What's that noise?" the shepherd asked.

"What you hear is the voices of others who have also sought refuge from the floods," the second llama told him. "Let's hurry or there'll be no room for us."

So they pushed on, climbing ever higher until they reached a small plateau just below the peak and saw that an extraordinary collection of birds and beasts had gathered. There were no other people, but there were bears and jaguars and monkeys and deer and foxes, as well as condors and parrots and hummingbirds and doves. It was strange to see, huddled side by side, creatures who ordinarily would never stay peacefully together, but they were all too frightened of the flood waters to attack one another.

The newcomers had not long joined them when

the sea began to rise. Higher and higher it rose until it had covered the forests and the plains and was still rising. For six days it rose, creeping ever closer until the spray from the waves blew in their faces and on the fur and feathers of the creatures crouching beside them, making them huddle even closer together, clinging to the very peak of the mountain.

By now there was no food left and everyone was hungry. How much longer would it be, the shepherd wondered, before the larger birds and animals attacked the smaller ones to satisfy their hunger? Even he began looking at the doves and thinking about pigeon pie, but he knew that Viracocha would be angry with any creature who turned against his fellow. Suddenly he noticed that the fox too was looking at the doves, his nose quivering. Before the shepherd could make a move, the fox turned to pounce but, as he did so, the tip of his tail dipped into the water lapping the side of the rock beneath him. There and then the tip of his tail turned black.

"Oh, my tail!" he cried, drawing back.

"That's a warning from Viracocha," bleated the first llama. "We must all stay friends or we'll be destroyed."

So the animals and birds, hungry though they were, left each other in peace. Soon after that, the flood waters started to fall back a little. For the next five days they kept on falling until the sea had returned to its bed. Then the shepherd and his family and all the birds and animals went back down the side of the mountain to begin their lives again, but they soon found everyone and everything else had been either drowned or swept away by the floods. People, houses, crops—all were gone, and there was nothing to eat but a few plants and roots still clinging to the soil.

The shepherd and his family collected driftwood which had been caught in crevices of the rocks, after they had been torn from the trees as they were washed away, and from this they built themselves a small shack. Soon, however, they had eaten every plant and root they could find, so the shepherd's two sons set out in search of food for the family. They travelled all day without finding anything to eat and, when darkness covered the land, they set up camp on high ground for the night.

Next day they set off to search once more, but again found nothing. When they returned to their camp, however, they cried out in surprise for set out in front of their makeshift tent was a feast. Every sort of delicacy that could be made from maize and beans and eggs and fruit had been prepared and served on palm leaf plates, with their favourite drink of *chicha* (a beer made from fermented corn) to wash it down.

They were so hungry that they did not wait to find out who had prepared such a wonderful meal, but fell upon it and ate every scrap. Afterwards, however, they looked around for a sign of people, but could find no one. Next day they again went hunting for, as the eldest son said, "Our father and mother will be very hungry by now, not having had the good fortune to feast as we did last night."

All the same, after hunting all day they again returned to their camp empty-handed. Then a shout of delight from the younger boy brought his elder brother hurrying to his side.

"It's happened again!" he cried. "Another feast is waiting for us and it's even finer than the first."

This time they ran around the camp before they ate, searching for traces of their mysterious host, but again they saw no one and heard nothing but the calling of parrots.

"Who can be doing this?" asked the elder brother, but the younger only laughed.

"Who cares," he cried, falling on his food with enthusiasm, "so long as we are lucky enough to enjoy the results?"

Five times the same thing happened. Then the elder brother could stand it no longer.

"I must know who is bringing this food," he said. "If we can only find out where it comes from we can get more to take back to our parents. While you hunt today I will stay here and see if I can find out who is bringing it."

So he hid himself and waited. After a while he heard parrot calls and saw two macaws flying towards his hiding place. When they dropped to the ground he saw, to his amazement, that they had the faces of young women. They began preparing a meal, but he could keep silent no longer. Running from his hiding place, he hurried towards the birds, but at once they flew away, chattering angrily, without leaving any food.

When the younger brother returned from his fruitless search, he was disappointed to find no food and asked his brother what had happened.

"Could you not have left well alone?" he cried, when the elder brother had told his story. "Now they may never bring us food again!"

For three days it seemed as if he might be right, for they went hungry. Then once again they returned to find food as before.

"Tomorrow I will hide again," the elder brother said, as he drained his *chicha*.

"And maybe anger the parrots again?" the younger one cried. "This time I will wait with you to make sure you don't spoil everything."

So next morning both brothers hid. After a while the two macaws flew over as before and began preparing a feast, but this time the younger brother held back the elder one until the meal was ready. Then, while the birds had their backs to them, laying out the food on the palm leaves, the two brothers stole up behind them and captured them. Immediately the two macaws turned into two beautiful Canarian girls.

So the two boys married them and learned where maize and beans and fruit and hens were still to be found. Then they not only took supplies back to their parents, but also took bean sprouts and fruit plants to replant the mountainside. The flood waters had made the ground fertile so these grew quickly and after that there was always food for everyone.

In time the two couples had six sons and six

daughters between them and from these are descended all the Canarians alive today. That is why the Canarians think of macaws as very special birds and wear their bright-coloured tail feathers in their hair at every festival.

ଓଓଓ

❖

The Scabby Man who Lit
Up the Sun

❖

Mexico

❖

A race known as the Aztecs in Mexico told a very different tale about the early days of the world. Known to other races as the People of the Sun, because they were sun-worshippers, they believed that there had been four suns before the one that shone on them and still shines on us today.

The first sun, they said, was called the Sun of the Four Jaguars and lasted for 676 years until the gods became angry at the wickedness of the people. Then they sent jaguars to kill and eat them all, and it sounds as if they must have eaten the sun too for it disappeared out of the sky at the same time. After that, the land was taken over by a race of giants.

The second sun, called the Sun of the Four Winds, lasted for 364 years, but then the people became foolish. They thought about nothing but enjoying themselves and, instead of working, spent their time eating and drinking and singing and dancing. Once again the gods grew impatient and sent winds to sweep the sun from the sky and the people from the face of the earth.

The third sun, called the Sun of the Four Fires, lasted for 312 years, but then the people began to forget the gods, believing that they themselves were all-powerful. In their anger, the gods allowed the sun to burn up and the earth to split open. The people fell down the cracks into the fires which raged at the centre of the earth, while erupting volcanoes poured boiling lava down on to them from the tops of all the mountains. Anybody who managed to escape by leaping high into the air was turned into a bird.

Before making the fifth sun, the gods gathered together in the darkness to decide what to do.

"People don't deserve to have a sun," one said. "We've given them four already and look how they've behaved!"

"But there *must* be a sun," argued another. "Without the sun nothing will grow."

"Besides," added a third, "I hate it when it's dark. It's depressing and I can't see what I'm doing."

So in the end they made a fifth sun and set it in place in the sky.

"Now," said the first god, "all we have to do is to light it up."

"Maybe if the people lit it up themselves," the second suggested, "they might feel as if it were their responsibility to look after it. Then they might take better care of it instead of behaving so badly that we have to keep destroying it and making new ones."

"But a man couldn't light up the sun without killing himself," said the third. "Its heat would burn him up."

"And yet it would be a great honour," the first argued. "Let's see if anyone will offer to do it."

So the gods sent word throughout all the land that whoever lit up the fifth sun would be remembered for ever and volunteers should apply within four days. For three days nobody came. Then, on the fourth day, a splendid person presented himself before the gods.

He wore a coat made from hummingbird feathers in brilliant reds, blues, greens and yellows, while around his neck hung many necklaces of turquoise beads strung on bands of gold. He was a big, powerful man with the grand manner of somebody very rich and he had a loud, booming voice.

"My name is Tecciztecatl of the Sea-Shell," he boomed, "and if you grant me the honour of lighting the sun I'll give many fine presents to the gods. I've precious feathers plucked from the tail of the sacred quetzal bird, fine stone flints sharpened to a perfect cutting edge and needles of beautiful red coral, better than any you will find elsewhere."

"Very well," he was told. "Since no one else has applied, you have the job. Do penance for four days and then you may approach the sacred fire."

Tecciztecatl had hardly gone away to start his fasting and praying when a shabby little man appeared before the gods. He wore a rough jacket made out of rushes and bark torn from a tree, while his face was covered in ugly looking spots.

"What has a scabby little man like you got to offer?" the first god asked him scornfully.

"I've several bundles of green reeds," he replied in a quiet little voice.

"And do you imagine that's enough to give in return for the honour of lighting up the sun?" sneered the second god.

"I'm afraid I've got nothing else," answered Nanautzin, for that was the little man's name, "except for my own blood and skin. You can have those if you like."

"How can you give us your own blood and skin," asked the third god, "and still live afterwards to light up the sun?"

"I can give you my blood by pricking myself on a sharp thorn," Nanautzin replied. "As for my skin, I can give you the scabs off my spots."

"Yuk!" exclaimed the first god in disgust. "D'you think gods want such horrible things?"

"Send him away, him and his nasty old scabs!" shouted the second god, but the third looked thoughtful.

"The poor man has offered us everything he has," he told the others. "These things, nasty though they may be, are more of a sacrifice for him than all the feathers, flints and corals offered by Tecciztecatl."

The first and second gods both pulled faces, but they could not disagree.

"Very well," said the first. "Let him also do penance for four days and then we will decide who is the fittest to light up the sun."

So Nanautzin, like Tecciztecatl, went away to fast and pray for four days. In the meantime, the gods built a huge fire on a raised platform at the foot of the pyramid we know today as the Temple of the Sun at Teotihuacan. Four days later, just before midnight, both men were brought to the temple and led up the hundreds of steps to the top of the 215-foot-high pyramid.

"Now," said the first god to Tecciztecatl, who had pushed proudly forward to the head of the little procession, "the hour of your glory has arrived. Go ahead and light up the sun."

"How?" he asked, looking out across the Valley of Mexico far below him, still shrouded in darkness.

"By casting yourself into the fire, of course," the second god said casually.

Tecciztecatl took a step back from the edge of the flat-topped pyramid in horror.

"Is there no other way?" he gasped.

The third god shook his head.

"Only a human torch can light the fire of the fifth sun, so that it may shine on earth and give it life," he said gently. "That's why your name and the sacrifice of your life will be remembered for ever."

Tecciztecatl clenched his fists and stepped forward until he was again standing on the edge of the pyramid. Smoke from the great fire below rose up like a storm cloud, making his eyes smart. Catching his breath and choking, he stepped back a second time.

"Would you rather I went first?" a quiet little voice asked politely from behind him and, turning, he saw Nanautzin standing as if meekly awaiting his turn in the queue.

"Certainly not!" snapped Tecciztecatl, drawing his splendid cloak away from the ugly little man as if he were afraid that his poverty might be catching.

Once again he stepped forward so that he stood on the very edge of the great pyramid and looked down. He could see the flames leaping higher and higher and, far above them though he was, he could feel the great heat rising from them. Gasping, he stepped back a third time.

"Come," cried the first god impatiently. "Make haste to jump or the flames will die down and there is no more timber to throw on it. We have already cut down every tree in the valley to get enough wood. You asked for this honour, so don't keep the gods waiting any longer."

Once more Tecciztecatl stepped forward. He could hear the crackling of the flames below as the wind tossed little sparks from the fire high into the air. One of these touched his bare arm, burning it and Tecciztecatl thought that, if a tiny spark could be so painful, the agony of becoming a human torch must be unimaginable. A cold sweat broke out on his forehead and he felt faint. He must have staggered backwards because he suddenly became aware of Nanautzin standing between him and the edge.

"May I?" he was asking politely.

"Very well, Scabby One," replied the second god. "Let you be the one to light up the sun."

Nanautzin smiled and his smile lit up his ugly little face like sunshine, until it was no longer ugly. Then he hurled himself down from the top of the pyramid. As he fell into the flames, the bark and rushes of his clothing caught fire, lighting up like a great torch which blazed across the sky. It burnt so fiercely that everyone had to shield their eyes from it and, only when it finally burnt out, did they see a fiery orb slowly rising above the pyramid.

"The Scabby One has himself become the light of the sun," the third god said solemnly. "Now he will no longer be thought of as ugly, but will be worshipped as one of the gods."

Tecciztecatl felt a terrible shame. Was a poor little man like Nanautzin to be honoured for ever for his courage, while his own name would become a symbol of cowardice? Gathering himself together, he did not give himself time to think any more about what he was doing, but leaped from the pyramid into the now dying embers of the fire.

His feathered cloak flickered with a silvery light as the faint bluish flames of his torch barely rose above the Earth's surface. Yet, when that light too had gone, a pale silvery orb was seen, hanging just above the horizon. Later that day, as the blazing sun sank slowly in front of the pyramid, casting a red glow across the valley, the pale silvery orb began to rise into the sky in its place.

"Tecciztecatl has become the light of the moon," the third god said. "Let us now build a lesser pyramid nearby, as a Temple to the Moon for, as he of the Sea-Shell followed the Scabby One in sacrifice, so the moon will always follow the sun in its path across the sky."

❧❧❧

❖

Glooscap and the Giant

❖

North America

❖

O nce upon a time there was a little village on the coast of what is now the state of Maine in the north-east of the United States of America. In that village there lived a Passamaquoddy tribe who spent their days happily in hunting and fishing. Indeed, even their name comes from the words "Peskede makadi", which means "plenty of pollock". But, although they had the whole of the great Atlantic Ocean in which to fish and swim, they had only the one small stream of pure, clean water for drinking, so they were in a terrible fix when one day the stream ran dry.

They thought at first that when the rains came in the autumn the water would flow once more, but it never did. Even when the snow melted in the spring and water dripped off the woodland trees until the ground underneath them became a swamp, there was nothing in the bed of the stream but a nasty green slime. By now the people were all very worried, so they gathered outside the chief's wigwam to discuss the problem.

"What are we going to do?" they asked the chief. "We can't live without water."

"I'll send a scout to trace the stream back to its source," he told them. "Somewhere between here and the place where the water bubbles up out of the ground, something must have happened to stop the water flowing. He will find out what's wrong and put it right."

So the man the chief had picked for the task set off along the empty bed of the stream. He walked for a very long time until he saw ahead of him a village much like his own. When he reached it, however, he saw that the people were not at all like his own tribe. In fact they were not like any people he had ever seen before, because their feet were webbed like a duck's and their hands too.

By now the stream was wider than it was at his own village and there was a little water in it, but it was very dirty-looking and it smelled nasty. After walking all day the man was thirsty, so he asked the people with webbed hands and feet if he could have some water to drink.

"You must ask our chief," they told him. "Even we can only get water by asking him and he never gives us as much as we need."

"Where will I find him?" the man asked.

"Further up stream," they said, so the man continued on his way.

After a while he heard a loud splashing and, looking up, saw a terrifying sight. Bathing in a large pool further upstream was a truly hideous giant. Like his tribe, he had webbed hands and feet. He also had a great swollen body, a huge grinning mouth running from ear to ear, and yellow eyes which stood out from his face like headlamps on a car. He was so enormous that it was only from where he first saw him that the man could see both his hands and his feet. As soon as he got closer, the giant's head was so far above him that he could no longer see it.

What he could see, quite clearly, was the reason why their stream had dried up. The giant had dug a huge hole in it to make a swimming-pool big enough even for him and had dammed the stream so that the water flowed into the pool but no further. While the man was still thinking about this, he heard a loud, threatening, croaking sort of voice coming from far above him.

"What do you want, you silly little man?" it croaked.

Shaking with fright, the man plucked up his courage and shouted up to where he knew the giant's head must be. "I'm from a village further down-stream," he cried at the top of his voice, "and the water has dried up. Your swimming-pool is taking it all and that's not fair. We need it for drinking and you're only playing around in it!"

There was a terrible silence for what seemed to the man to be a very long time. Then a nasty laugh echoed down to him, followed by mocking words:

"What if I am?

I don't care!

If you want water

Go elsewhere!"

"But the people are dying of thirst!" the man called out boldly, and this time the answer came back right away in an angry croak.

"Let them die,
They shan't have a sup!
Now go away
Or I'll swallow you up!"

Then, to his horror, the man suddenly saw an enormous head coming towards him from above. The giant was stooping over him, his great mouth wide open. A long black tongue flicked out from it and began to wind itself around the man. At that he hesitated no longer but, twisting away before the tongue could grip him in a noose, he ran as fast as he could all the way back to his village. The people all hurried out of their wigwams when they heard him coming.

"Well?" they all cried. "Did you find out what has happened to our water?"

"I did," the man gasped, "and there was nothing I could do to put it right. A giant has taken it all to swim in and, if we complain, he'll eat us all alive!"

At that the people turned away and went sadly back into their wigwams to wait for death. But there was someone who knew all about their misfortunes and was planning to do something about it, and that someone was Glooscap.

Now Glooscap was known to all the woodland tribes of the north-east, even though they had never actually met him. He had, after all, taught their great-

great-grandfathers all they knew, from the names of the stars to the way to paint pictures, make useful and attractive things, hunt, fish, grow crops and make medicines from herbs. It was said that he looked and spoke like an ordinary man and had come from a country far away to the east, but everyone knew he was no ordinary mán, for he knew everything that happened in the world, even before it happened. Now he knew that the people were suffering through no fault of their own and he decided to help them.

He prepared himself for battle, just as one of the Passamaquoddy tribe would do, painting his body red and drawing yellow circles around his eyes. He hung a large shell from each ear and made himself a headdress out of black and white eagle feathers. Then he used a magic spell to make himself twice the height of a man, tore a great slab of flint from the mountainside to use as a knife and set out for the village of the people with webbed hands and feet. The earth trembled beneath his feet and his war cries echoed from the mountainside like thunder as he covered the distance in a few mighty strides.

"I want water for the village downstream!" he roared at the people, who stood shivering with fear at the sight of him.

"We only have a muddy trickle ourselves," they stammered, "but you're welcome to that if you want it."

"That won't do," Glooscap thundered. "I want clean water running in the stream every day, the way it used to do."

And he strode on until he came face to face with the giant.

"Tear down that dam until the water flows clear again," he ordered angrily.

The giant glared at him, blinking his bulging eyes. Then he replied in his loud, croaking voice:

"All that water
Belongs to me,
Now go away
Or I'll eat you for tea!"

"Oh, you will, will you?" roared Glooscap. "We'll soon see about that!"

The giant opened his enormous mouth to swallow Glooscap but then he got a surprise. Glooscap began to grow bigger and bigger until he was taller than the tallest tree in the forest and even his arm was too big to fit into the giant's mouth. Then he seized his flint knife and stuck it into the giant's great fat stomach. At once water began to pour out of it in a great river which burst the giant's dam as it thundered on its way towards the Passamaquoddy village and on to the sea.

"That should give the people water," laughed Glooscap, "and now I'll deal with you!"

By now, with all the water that had flowed out of his body, the giant had got a lot smaller, and soon he was so small that his head only came up to Glooscap's waist, but Glooscap was still not satisfied. He grabbed the shrinking giant with both hands and began to squeeze him. He squeezed and squeezed until he was smaller than a man's hand, and the more

Glooscap squeezed, the more his skin wrinkled and his eyes bulged. Then Glooscap turned him around to face the mud where once his swimming-pool had been.

"Now hop it!" he roared, and the poor little wrinkled thing hopped.

He kept on hopping until he reached the safety of the rushes and hid himself amongst them, for he had become the first bullfrog.

❖

The Swallowing Monster

❖

Southern Africa

❖

About the same time, in what is now Lesotho in the south of Africa, there was a terrible monster called Kammapa. It was a huge, shapeless creature which looked as if it were made of rubber and seemed to change shape from day to day. Sometimes there would be a bulge on the right side of its body and sometimes on the left.

Sometimes there would be a strange lump in its back and sometimes in its front, while sometimes it seemed to have bulges and lumps everywhere. But no matter how funny it looked, no one ever laughed at it, for it was a fearsome monster that sucked up every living thing it came across the way a vacuum cleaner sucks up dust. Soon there was only one village left in the whole of Africa.

It was a small village of little mud huts in the middle of a beautiful sunny valley high up in the mountains. Hens pecked around the huts, dogs scratched themselves in the heat, goats grazed wherever they could find anything growing and little black children played in the sandy soil while their mothers worked in the maize and wheat fields and their fathers drove their cows to and from the mountain pastures. Then one day the monster silently bulged and oozed its way through the high mountain pass and down into the little village, swallowing up everything in sight: hens, dogs, goats, cows, children, mothers and fathers alike.

Right at the end of the village, however, there was one woman who saw the monster coming. She happened to be beside the ash pit, so she smeared herself from head to foot with the ashes and then lay down on the ground, keeping absolutely still. When the monster had sucked up every other living thing, he reached the ash pit, but the woman looked like ashes and smelled like ashes, so he oozed and bulged his way back again towards the mountain pass.

With all the people and animals and birds that he had swallowed, however, he was now twice as fat as he had been when he arrived. He had lumps and bumps everywhere, back, front and sides, so he was too big to squeeze himself through the narrow pass. He felt far too comfortably full and sleepy to worry about that, so he lay down to have his after-dinner nap. In a few minutes the whole valley shook with the sound of his snoring.

While he was sleeping peacefully, the woman who had hidden herself beside the ash pit gave birth to a baby boy. Round his neck when he was born she found a leather thong from which hung a tooled leather medallion that showed he was under the protection of the god Lituolone, so his mother named him after the god. But babies are not usually born wearing anything at all, let alone signs that they are under the protection of a god, so the woman may have suspected there was something rather unusual about her baby. Even so, she never expected anything like the extraordinary thing that happened next. In the two or three minutes that it took her to fetch a little basket to use as a temporary cradle for the baby, he grew into a full-sized man. You can imagine how surprised she was when she hurried back with her basket to see this man sitting there, where the baby had been, with a spear in one hand and a hunting-knife in the other.

"What have you done with my baby?" she cried in alarm, looking all around her, for she never dreamed she could be talking to him.

"I *am* your baby," he told her, "but why are there no other people in the village? I can see no men, no children and no women but you, and I can't even see any birds or animals."

"That's because the monster Kammapa has eaten them all," his mother told him, "and he would have eaten me too only I fooled him by disguising myself. He's asleep now, but I'm afraid as soon as he wakes up again he'll find us both and eat us too."

"Oh no he won't!" cried Lituolone. "Just show me where he is and I'll deal with him."

So his mother led him around the corner until he could see the huge creature, bulging in every direction, with its mouth ajar, snoring.

"That's Kammapa!" she told him.

"Then Kammapa is about to get his come uppance!" Lituolone laughed, sharpening his spear on a stone.

The woman was naturally afraid for him, but she hoped he might plunge his spear into the monster while it was still asleep. At Lituolone walked towards it, however, its eyes opened wide and it gave a great belch. Then it saw Lituolone and lumbered to an upright position, its mouth wide open, ready to swallow him whole, but Lituolone was too quick for it. He dodged to one side and, as Kammapa lunged past him, he attacked it from behind, trapping it in the narrow neck of the mountain pass. Then he stabbed it with his spear and the great shapeless thing shook like a jelly, made a glugging sound and fell down dead.

Lituolone took his hunting knife then and stuck it into the monster's front, meaning to cut it up. To his amazement, however he heard a man's voice crying out:

"Oh, you've wounded me!"

Startled, he pulled out the knife and instead stuck it into the monster's back, but immediately he heard a woman's voice.

"Take care," it cried, "or you'll cut my arm!"

Again Lituolone pulled out the knife and stuck it into the monster's right side, but this time he heard a child's voice.

"Please don't hurt me!" it cried, so Lituolone pulled out the knife once more and tried the left side instead.

He had hardly done so, however, before he heard a dog howling inside the monster's body. Amazed, he carefully tried one part of its body after another, but every time he heard a man or a woman or a child cry out, or a dog howl or a goat bleat or a cow moo or a hen cackle in alarm. So there was nothing for it but to put down his hunting knife, force wide the monster's mouth and climb inside it. Then he pushed and pulled at its rubbery skin until he had succeeded in turning it inside out.

Then he saw the most extraordinary sight for, out of that monster tumbled hundreds of living people, animals and birds. Men and women, boys and girls, cocks and hens, dogs, goats and cows crawled and rolled, jumped and fell from the skin of Kammapa until the dead monster was nothing but skin. All the lumps and bulges that had made him look so fat had been living creatures that he had swallowed. Then you can imagine the excitement as families found each other and kissed and hugged, rejoicing at their freedom.

"Thank you, thank you!" they all cried to Lituolone.

"Only for him we'd still be no more than bulges inside Kammapa!" shouted one.

"Let's make him our chief!" suggested another.

"Yes! Yes!" everyone cried, before collecting their dogs and hens and goats and cows and going back to their homes to start their lives once more.

Later they built Lituolone a fine big hut and brought him presents of dogs and goats and chickens and cows until he was the richest man in Africa.

All the girls thought he was wonderful, so he had no difficulty in finding himself a wife when the time came and they lived very happily for a while, but then things in the village changed.

There was one man who, far from thinking that Lituolone was wonderful, had nothing but complaints about him. He was the man who had first cried out when he was wounded by Lituolone's knife and he never stopped moaning about his injury. Long after the wound in his leg had completely healed, he was still grumbling about it.

"It's all very well for you," he would say to the others when they praised Lituolone, "but your great hero nearly crippled me!"

At first no one took much notice of him, but life is never good for everyone all the time. Sometimes the rain would be late in coming and the crops would fail from the drought. Sometimes the hens would not lay or the cows would give no milk. Then everyone would be hungry and perhaps a child would become sick and die. And whenever anything like that happened, the man whose leg Lituolone had wounded would seize the chance to blame him.

"Our fine chief does nothing to prevent these things happening," he would say, "despite the fact that he's supposed to be such a wonder!"

In the end he managed to stir up trouble among the people and they decided to get rid of their chief. They made plan after plan. First they dug a big pit not far from his hut and covered it with grass so that he would not see it. Then they all sat back and waited for him to fall into it and die. When the shaft of Lituolone's spear suddenly went down into the hole, however, he had the good sense not to follow it.

Then one day, when they were all out on a three-day hunting trip, the people lit a great fire in the mouth of the cave in which Lituolone was sleeping, thinking that he would be trapped inside and would suffocate from the smoke. They got the fire burning nicely and waited to hear him choking and gasping. Instead, they found that he was standing amongst them outside the cave.

Then they decided to push him off a cliff. One man suddenly rushed at him from behind when he was standing near the edge but, just at that very moment, Lituolone moved to one side and the man hurtled over the cliff himself. Lituolone looked over the edge and saw him lying, badly hurt, on a rock half-way down the cliff face and it was he who climbed down, rescued him and nursed him back to health.

After that, the people gave up trying to kill him. It would be nice if I could say that they gave up grumbling as well but, while there was clearly something miraculous about Lituolone, who grew from a newborn baby to a man in a few minutes and seemed to be protected by a god from every threat and danger, the others were only ordinary people like you and me and ordinary people are bound to grumble now and then.

❦❦❦

Other Books by
Carolyn Swift

Irish Myths & Tales for Young People
European Myths & Tales
Robbers in the House
Robbers in the Hills
Robbers in the Town
Robbers in the Theatre
Robbers on TV
Robbers in the Streets
Robbers in a Merc
Bugsy Goes to Limerick
Bugsy Goes to Cork
Bugsy Goes to Galway
The Secret City
The Mystery of the Mountain

And for Adults

Stage by Stage, Theatre Memoirs